My name is not Refugee

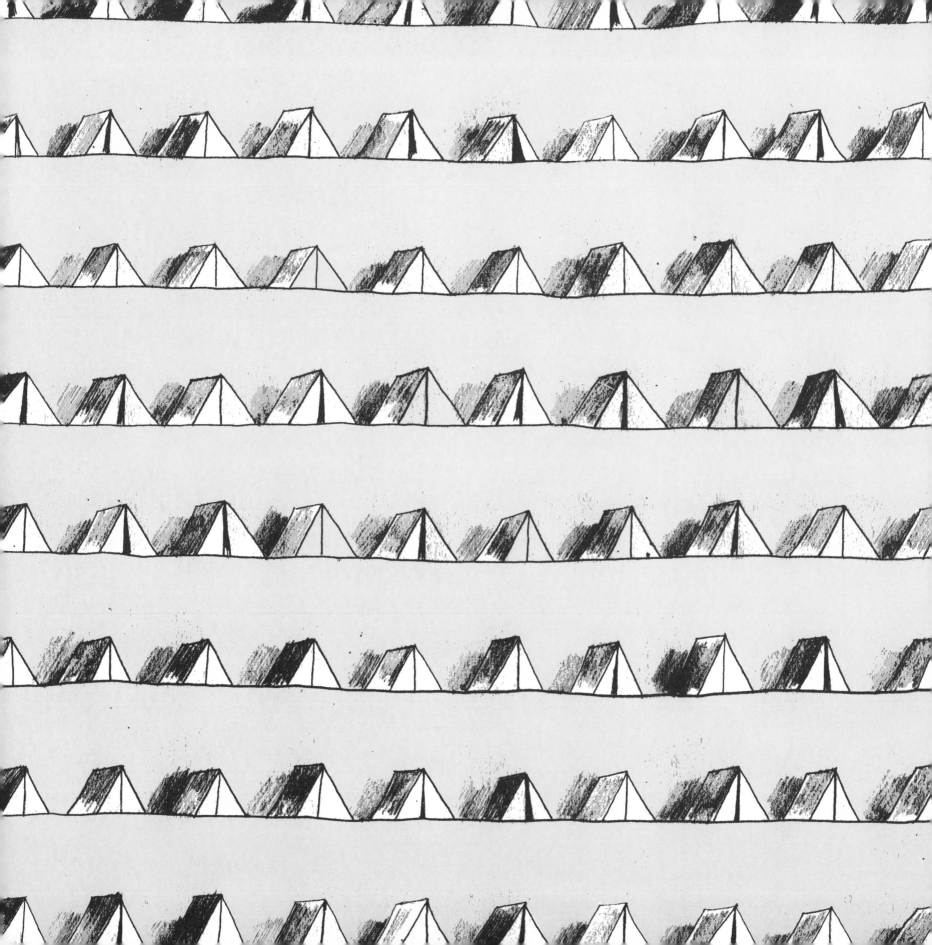

For Rosie, Frankie and John

First published in 2017 in Great Britain by
The Bucket List, an imprint of Barrington Stoke
18 Walker Street, Edinburgh, EH3 7LP

www.bucketlistbooks.co.uk

Text & Illustrations © 2017 Kate Milner

A CIP catalogue record for this book is available
from the British Library upon request

ISBN: 978-1-911370-06-2

Printed in Turkey

Kate Milner

My name is not Refugee

We have to leave this town, my mother
told me, it's not safe for us, she said.

Shall I tell you what it will be like?

We'll have to say goodbye to old friends.

You can pack your own bag, but remember,
only take what you can carry.

What would
you take?

We'll say goodbye to our town.

It will be a bit sad but quite exciting too.

Do you think you could live in a place where there is no water in the taps and no one to pick up the rubbish?

We'll march and dance and skate

and run and walk and walk and walk

and wait and wait and wait

and get up again and walk and walk ...

How far could you walk?

Sometimes we will be by ourselves.

It might get a bit boring.

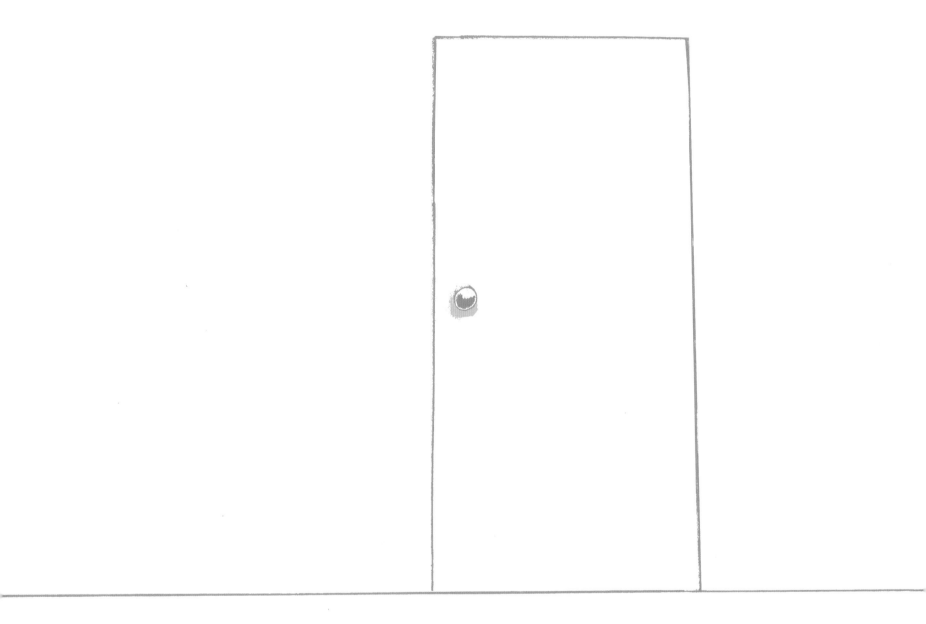

What games can
you think of?

Sometimes we will be with other people.

Do you always hold on to an adult's hand when you should?

We will see lots of new and interesting things.

Do you like cars and lorries?

We'll sleep in some strange places.

Where would you brush
your teeth or change
your pants?

We'll hear words we don't understand.

Can you speak more than one language?

And taste new foods.

What is the weirdest food
you have ever eaten?

We'll get to a place where we are
safe and we can unpack.

What things would
remind you of your
old home?

And soon those strange words
will start to make sense.

You'll be called Refugee
but remember
Refugee is not your name.

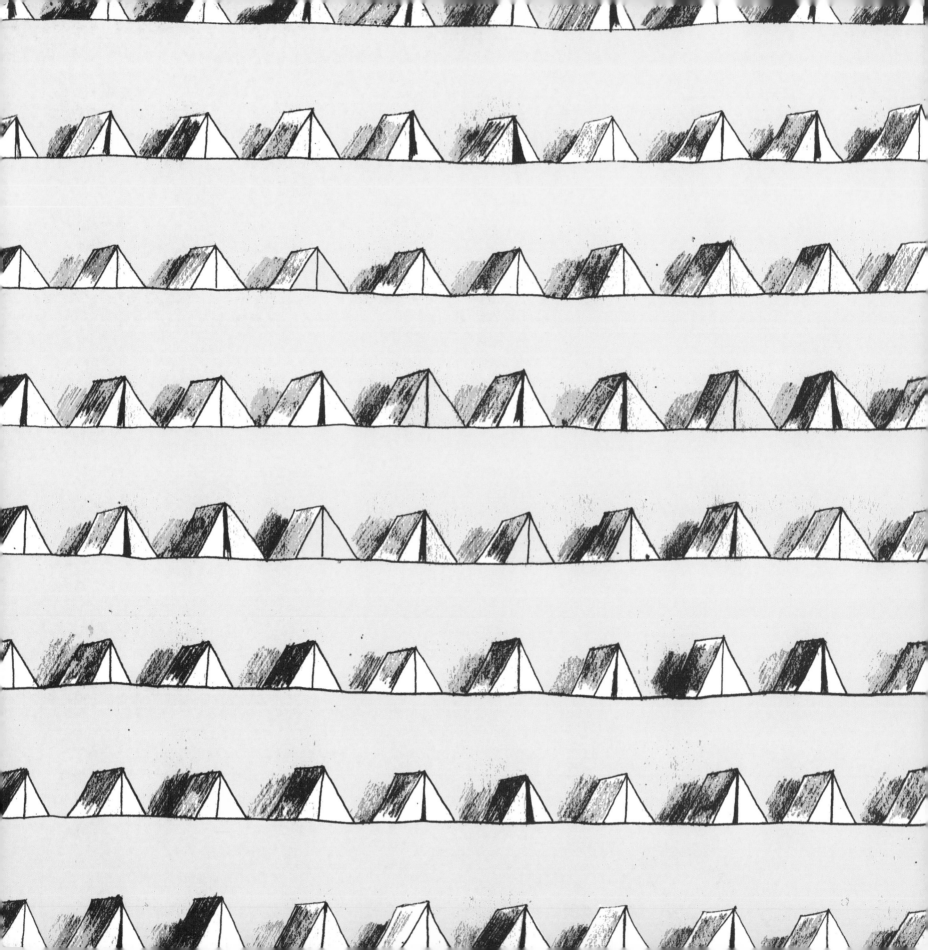